MARVEL

THOR
RAGNAROK

MARVEL

marvelkids.com

© 2017 MARVEL

Illustrations by Ron Lim

Cover design by Elaine Lopez-Levine. Cover illustration by Ron Lim.

Little, Brown and Company
Hachette Book Group
1290 Avenue of the Americas, New York, NY 10104
Visit us at LBYR.com
marvelkids.com

First Edition: October 2017

Little, Brown and Company is a division of Hachette Book Group, Inc.
The Little, Brown name and logo are trademarks of Hachette Book Group, Inc.

The publisher is not responsible for websites (or their content) that are not owned by the publisher.

ISBNs: 978-0-316-41390-9 (pbk.), 978-0-316-41387-9 (ebook), 978-0-316-41389-3 (ebook), 978-0-316-41386-2 (ebook)

Printed in the United States of America

CW

10 9 8 7 6 5 4 3 2 1

MARVEL
THOR
RAGNAROK
INTO THE FIRE

Adapted by R. R. Busse

Illustrations by Ron Lim

Based on the Screenplay by Eric Pearson

Story by Craig Kyle & Christopher Yost and Eric Pearson

Produced by Kevin Feige, p.g.a.

Directed by Taika Waititi

Ⓛ Ⓑ

LITTLE, BROWN AND COMPANY

New York   Boston

Thor is the proud prince of Asgard. He is also an Avenger who has protected Midgard—also known as Earth—on many occasions. He wields the enchanted hammer Mjolnir, a powerful weapon that only the worthy can lift.

Right now, though, he is not in Asgard or even on Earth. Thor has no idea at all where he is.

Thor had been searching for the source of a terrible vision, and he still does not know anything—yet—about the evil and ancient Hela, or that she is the darkness he saw coming for Asgard.

Without Thor or his powerful father, Odin, there to stop Hela's invasion, many Asgardians will get hurt.

Eventually, Thor remembers how he came to this strange world and it all started on an even stranger world....

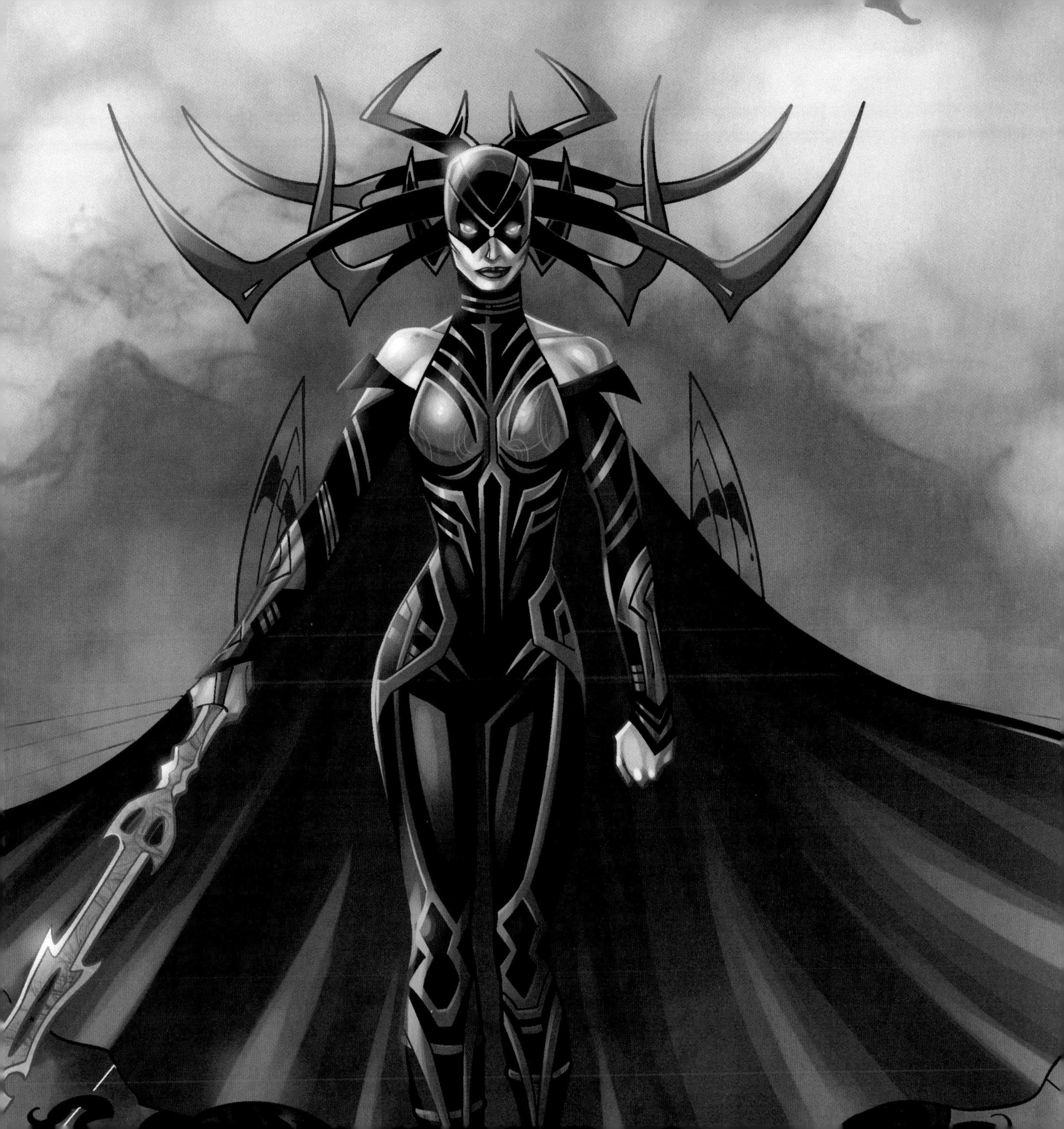

SOME TIME AGO...

Muspelheim is a realm full of fire and ruled by a powerful demon. Things are not going well for the Asgardian prince.

While visiting to find answers about the dark vision, Thor was captured by Surtur, a giant demon made of flame and rage.

Surtur gloats, threatening to bring a bound Thor back to Asgard and destroy the entire realm. Thor simply grins. "I see no reason for you to smile, son of Odin," Surtur growls. "You have no hope of escape."

A pounding echoes through the huge room. The booming comes closer and closer. Surtur's eyes widen. "What is that sound?"

Thor's own eyes shine happily, and, having finally freed himself from his chains, he holds out his arm. "Hope." Mjolnir bursts into the room!

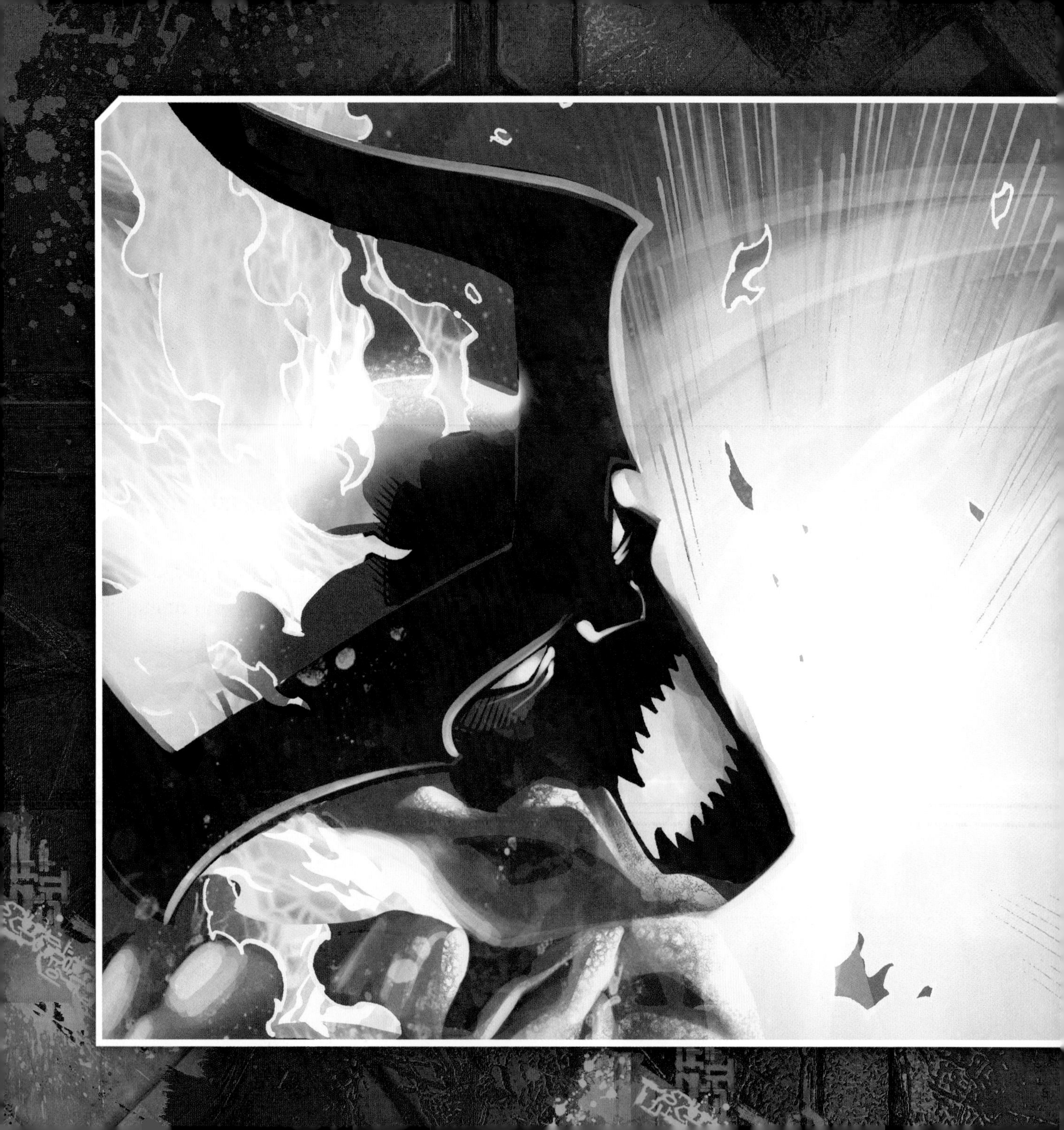

Thor is ready for battle now!
With a yell, he leaps into the fight.
CRACK!
"You wish to return to Asgard,
demon? I shall bring you myself!"
he says, relishing the combat.
Surtur falls back.

Instead of waiting for the counterattack, Thor strikes again while the demon lord is getting back on his feet. With another mighty blow from his hammer to Surtur's knees, Thor defeats his foe.

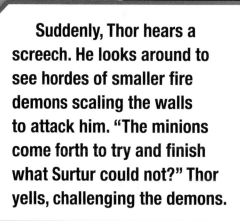

Suddenly, Thor hears a screech. He looks around to see hordes of smaller fire demons scaling the walls to attack him. "The minions come forth to try and finish what Surtur could not?" Thor yells, challenging the demons.

Looking up, Thor yells to an unseen friend. "Heimdall! The Bifrost, please," he says, expecting the usual beam of rainbow energy to transport him home. "Heimdall? Heimdall?" No bridge is coming to save him. Thor has to fight once more.

After defeating his many foes, Thor stands alone, no worse for the wear. Using Mjolnir to burst through the roof of Surtur's lair, Thor finds no help. Instead he finds… an enormous dragon, spewing flames!

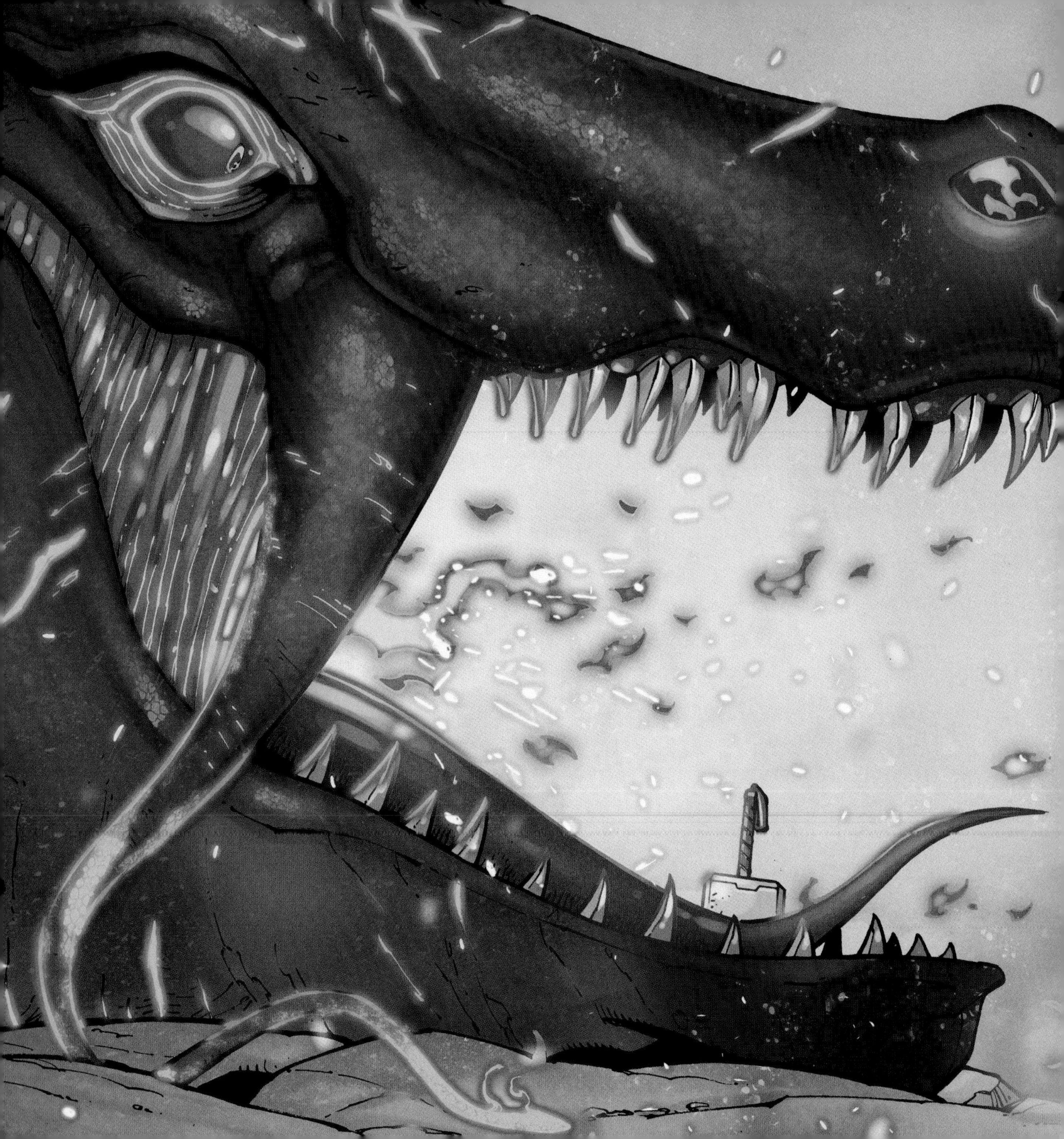

Thor dodges bursts of magical fire as he takes to the sky to escape the beast. The dragon follows. Thor catches the dragon off guard with a surprise attack, knocking the creature onto its white-hot belly.

As he places Mjolnir in the dragon's raging mouth, he calmly says, "Only those who are worthy may lift Mjolnir. Clearly, you are not worthy." The dragon is pinned by the enchanted hammer.

Back in Asgard, Thor's friend Heimdall was relieved of his duty to man the Bifrost. Instead, Skurge has taken on the important task, but he is not paying the slightest bit of attention to it. Instead, he is throwing a party to impress his friends.

Thor is still calling for a ride home, and he does not notice the dragon's deadly tail. *WHOOSH!*

Thor is knocked on his back and calls for Mjolnir. Free of the hammer, the dragon rears for another attack as Thor desperately yells for the Bifrost. It appears…*finally*!

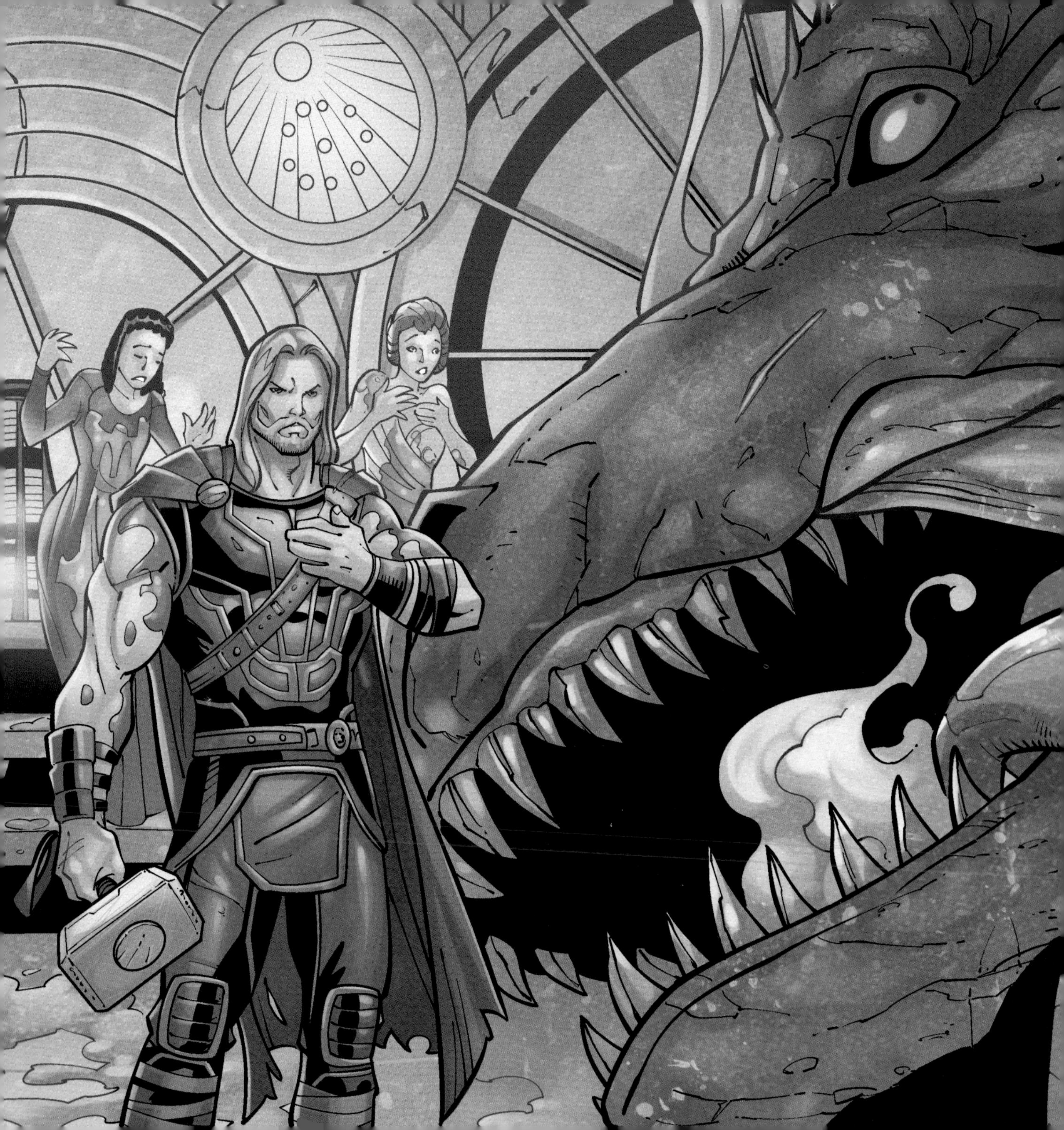

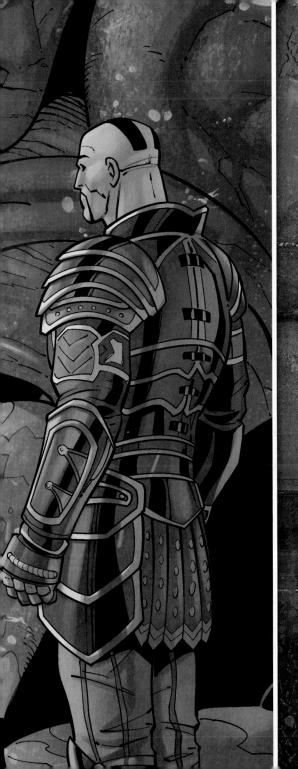

The Bifrost opens, and immediately, Thor comes flying through! But he is not alone: The dragon is in hot pursuit—for a second.

"Close it! The Bifrost! Now!" Thor bellows. The closing gate stops the dragon, but the beast scares away Skurge's party guests!

Thor knows something is wrong in Asgard. Skurge tells him that Thor's father, Odin, banished Heimdall. Thor is determined to find out what happened, and when Odin acts strangely, Mjolnir is able to pry an answer from him....

It turns out Thor's lying brother, Loki, has been acting as Odin while Thor was away. Thor is furious, and he makes Loki take him to their father.

Loki has hidden Odin on Earth, where no one in Asgard would think to look for him. Disguised as an ordinary human, Odin has no memory of being the king of Asgard.

Just as Thor (and Loki, after some rough persuading) begins taking Odin home on the Bifrost, a mysterious force ambushes them! Thor falls into blackness.

Now...

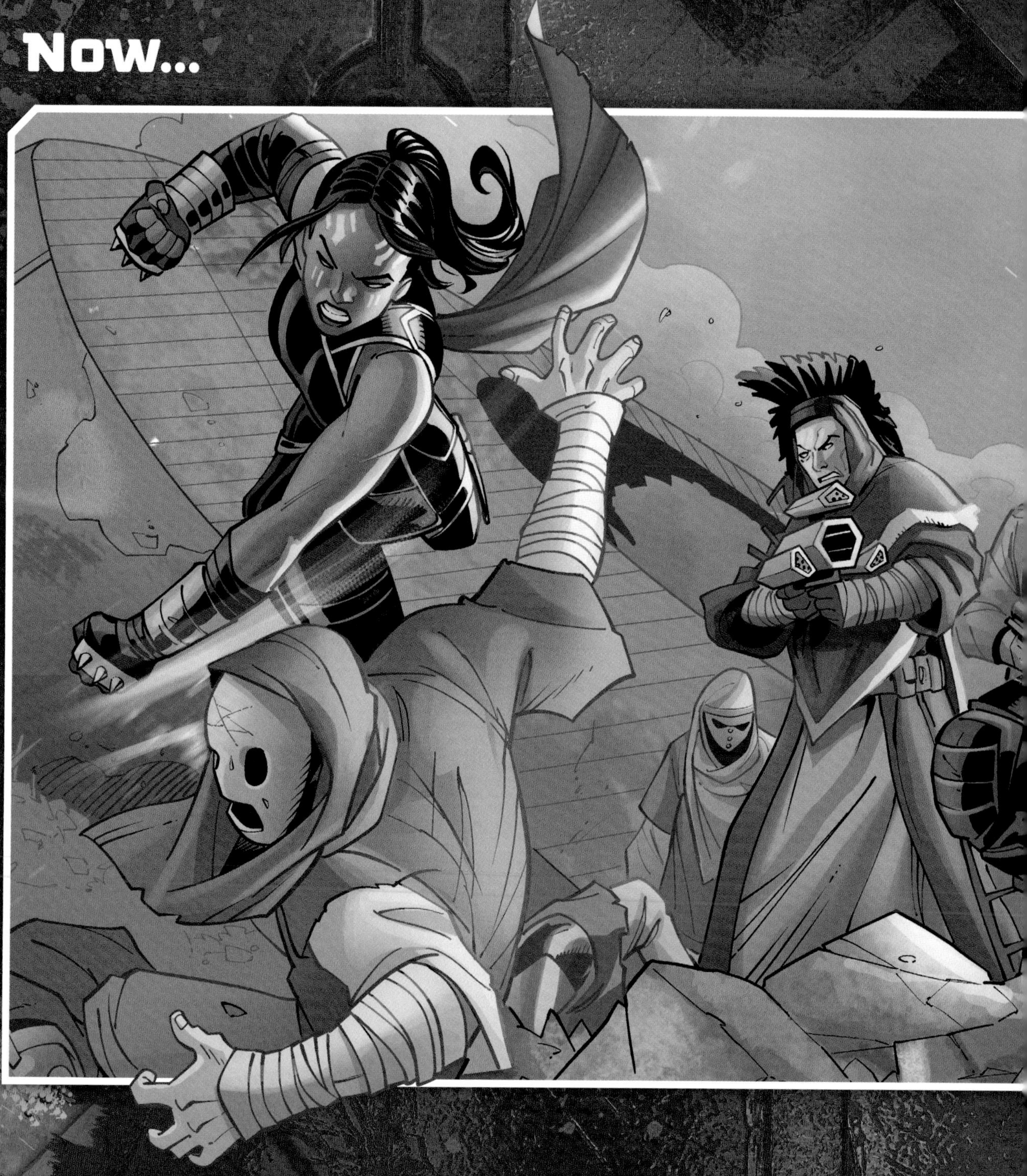

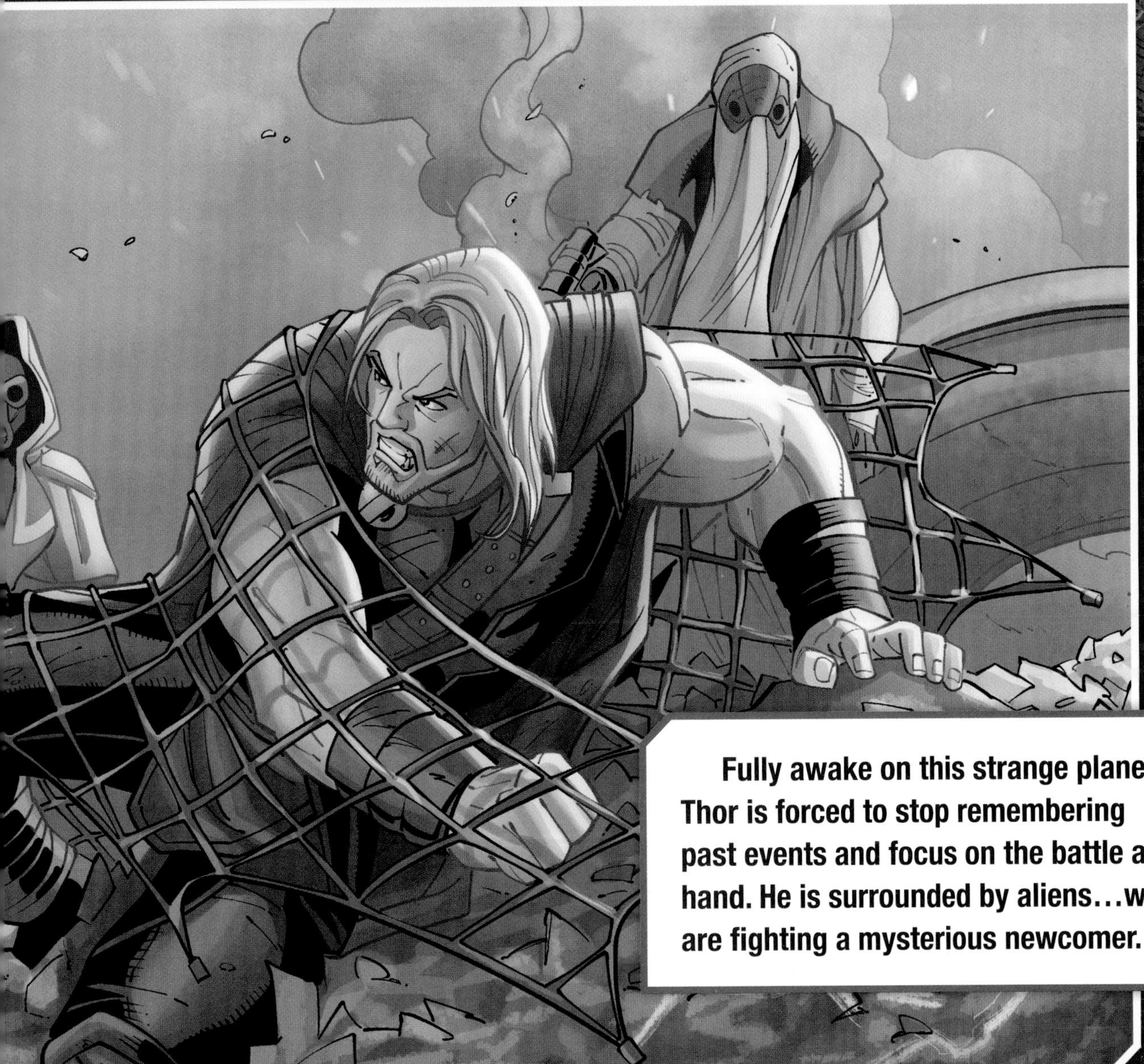
Fully awake on this strange planet, Thor is forced to stop remembering past events and focus on the battle at hand. He is surrounded by aliens…who are fighting a mysterious newcomer.

Victorious, the woman claims her prize. Her boss will pay good money to watch this Asgardian fight in the arena.

She delivers Thor to a man who calls himself the Grandmaster. The Grandmaster decides Thor *must* fight in his contest—he hasn't seen anyone this powerful since his current Champion.

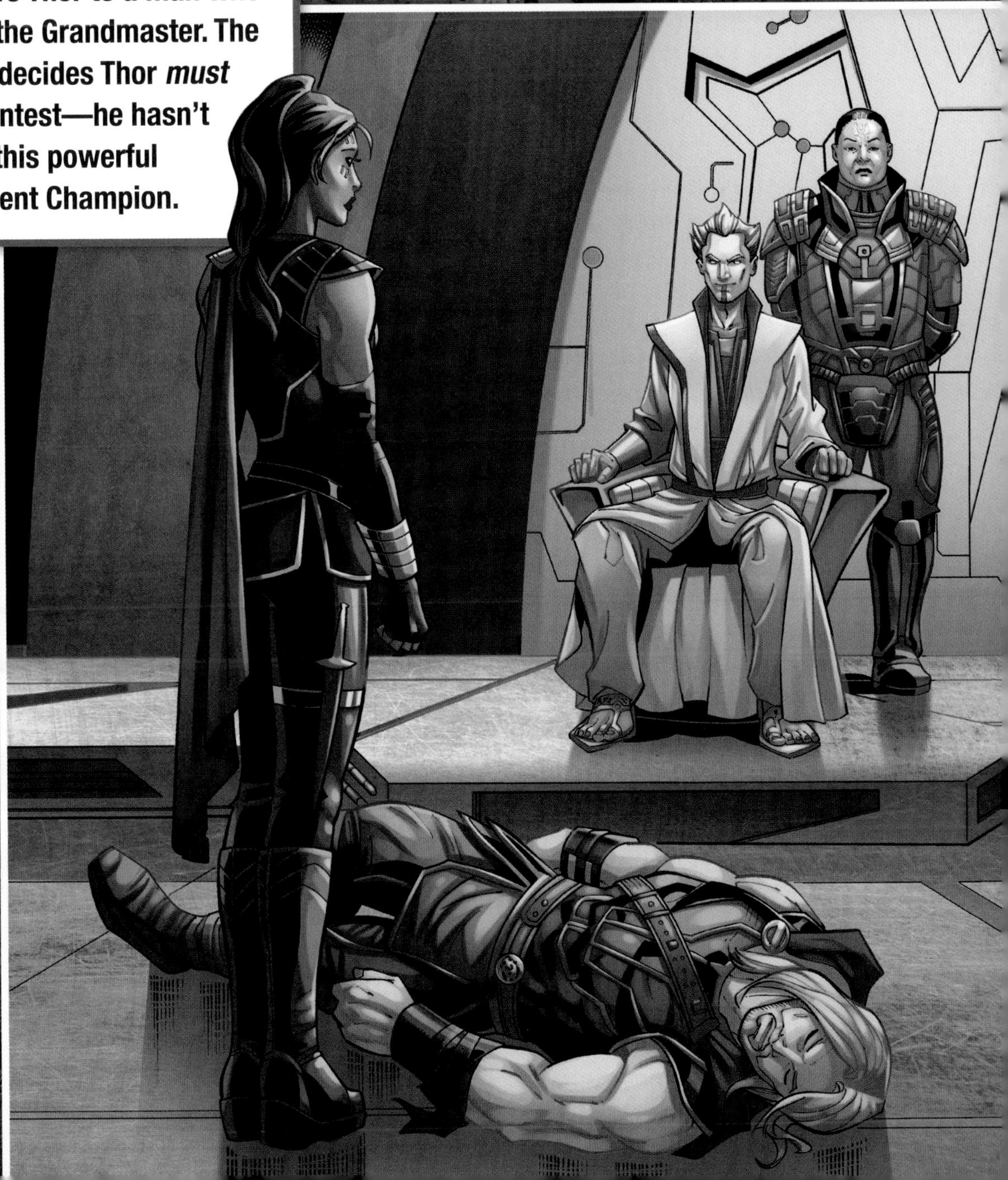

Of course…the current Champion is the Incredible Hulk: the strongest of all the Avengers. Thor will have to beat him in order to get home and save Asgard. He's in for the fight of his life!